THE MONSTER BOOK
FOR KIDS

MONSTROUS & MYTHICAL CREATURES FROM AROUND THE WORLD

BERNARD TATE

TOMOKAI RIVER

CONTENTS

INTRODUCTION

Vampires. Werewolves. Big Foot.

The Cactus Cat?

There are things in our world that aren't human. They aren't like normal animals, either. They are something else entirely, and they can be beautiful or ugly, frightening, or friendly. Creatures like this exist in every country in the world, in different stories and in different languages. No matter what they are called, however, they are all...monsters.

People have been telling stories about monsters since the beginning of time. You can find them in Greek mythology, and in the stories of the Ancient Egyptians, and in folktales from the furthest parts of Russia or China or Iceland, or even in your own back yard. Everywhere you go, there will always be tales to be told about creatures that defy description. What is it that fascinates us about monsters? Why do we love telling these tales? Why are there always more monsters to find and stories to tell?

Is it because monsters are scary? Is it because they're dangerous? Is it because some monsters are just a little bit weird?

Yes, yes, and yes.

Come along with me while I explore these monsters from all over the world, travelling the entire globe to find them wherever they might be hiding. In every country, there is a monster ready to help you, hurt you, or gobble you up! I've seen them all, and I've lived to tell you about it. You'll find creatures that you're probably familiar with, and some that you've never heard of before, but others you won't believe! I've even added a few tips about how to survive monster attacks, too.

I hope you have fun, and remember if you get too scared, you can always close the book. The monsters will be waiting for you when you come back!

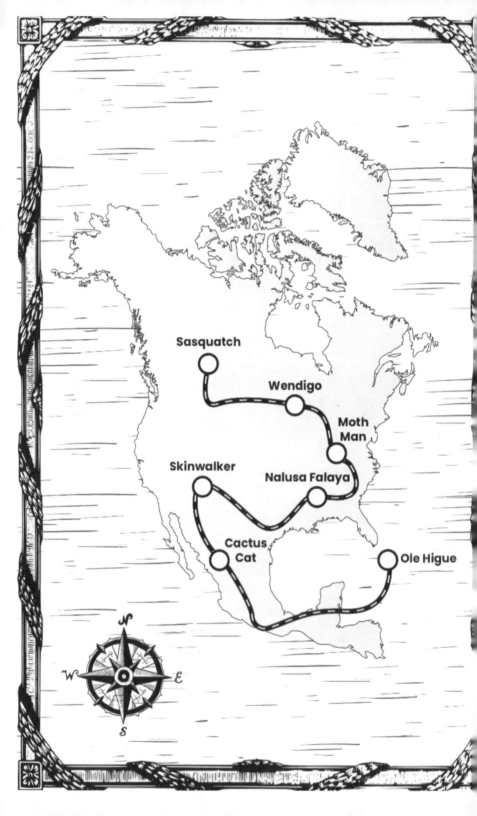

NORTH AMERICA

SASQUATCH

The sasquatch is a monster who has been seen many times in British Columbia in Canada, and in the northwest forests of the United States. He goes by another name that many people know him by: Bigfoot.

He is a big, hairy creature who looks almost like a large man, or maybe more like a gorilla. He isn't very fast, and in fact he walks with a slow, lumbering kind of gait, as if he's got all the time in the world to get wherever it is he's headed. I suppose when you live in the forest, and don't ever have to go to work or school or worry about things like that, you really do have all the time in the world. He's been caught on camera a few times, although the images are usually blurry and hard to make out. That's why so many people still think he's fake.

That's the way he likes it, by the way. If you ever get the chance to ask him about it, he'll say he likes being a bit of a mystery. He likes hiding out in tall woods, waiting for hikers to trek by and take pictures of the scenery. Then he'll jump out and photobomb their shot. When the hiker gets home and checks their photos, there'll be a blurry image of a hulking brute in the background, hairy from head to big toes…but smiling and waving!

In the meantime, he guards the forest and takes care of it, helping young trees grow and keeping forest fires from spreading too quickly. Really nice guy. I've got him in my contacts list, if you ever want to send him a text message.

WENDIGO

The native peoples of the Americas were here long before anyone else. They saw firsthand all the creatures who used to live in the untamed wilderness that eventually became Canada and the United States. The Algonquins, who lived around the Great Lakes, tell us of a special monster called a wendigo.

This monster looks like an extremely thin, extremely tall person. Some of them are even as tall as a fully grown tree, though most of them are much smaller. They hide in forests by standing very still and pretending to be trees. Be careful when you're walking through the woods. That tree you lean up against might be a wendigo. It might be hungry. Wendigos have no lips but they have very long, very sharp teeth. They make a frightening noise through their teeth that sounds like a hissing snake. Listen very carefully when you're in the woods. That sound might be the only warning you get.

Once when I was on a hike in the Adirondack mountains, I heard that sound. I quickly hid behind a tree and froze. I made sure it was a tree first, and then I hid and watched. Another hiker came by who obviously didn't know the things I know about monsters. He walked right toward the hissing sound, and suddenly what he thought were branches above turned out to be arms that reached down for him.

The wendigo grabbed him and picked him up. It didn't eat him, though - it did something worse. With its evil power, it turned the poor hiker into another wendigo! The man screamed the whole time, but when it had finished, he just hissed through his long, sharp teeth.

Wendigos can be killed with a knife made of silver or iron, but I didn't have either with me. I ran away as fast as I could, vowing that next time I went hiking, I'd be carrying a silver knife, just in case.

MOTHMAN

This monster has only ever been seen in one place, a small town in West Virginia named Point Pleasant. It was first seen by a group of friends driving in their car. In the deep of night, they saw a figure standing in the middle of the road. It was seven feet tall, with huge eyes that were bright red and glowing.

They stopped, of course, but before they could figure out what to do, the monster spread its wide, papery wings, and flew into the sky. But then it followed their car for miles and miles.

The Mothman was seen again and again by many other people in town, though it never bothered anyone. It never attacked anyone or hurt anybody. There weren't even any reports of pets disappearing like you hear about with the presence of some monsters. He was there, and then he was gone.

But moths lay eggs, and those eggs hatch into ugly brown caterpillars, and the caterpillars make web-like cocoons. When the cocoons hatch, they become more moths.

I'm in the basement of an abandoned church, and I'm looking at a dozen cocoons as big as a man. It's hatching season. Soon, these will all become more moths, and the Mothman will fly again.

Lighting a match, I wonder, *should I let them live?*

NALUSA FALAYA

The Choctaw are a Native people from the woods of the Southeastern part of the United States. They have warned people for generations not to walk the woods at night. They know there is a monster who stalks its next victim among the trees.

I've never been one to keep out of places when people tell me to stay away. Sometimes, the only way to find the most interesting things in life is to go where you're told not to go. Sometimes, of course, it's smarter to stay home.

Tonight, I'm walking through the deep woods of Mississippi. I'm looking for a monster that looks like a tall, very thin man. He has teeny, tiny eyes, and pointed ears. He's hard to spot, though, because from head to toe he's as dark as a shadow. That's why he blends into the woods so well, and why he usually comes out at night. I figure I have the advantage, though. When the Choctaw first encountered the Nalusa Falaya, they didn't have things like flashlights. They hadn't been invented yet.

Thanks to modern technology, I have a flashlight that lights up the woods around me.

This monster likes to hide, and watch, and wait for children to cross his path. He'll jump out and scare them and send them running away in terror. If the person he finds is an adult, he'll stick a thorn in their hand. The thorn makes the person become bad. They begin stealing, and cheating their friends, and they can't stop.

This monster even crawls on its belly sometimes to make it harder for anyone to see it. As if it needs any more help sneaking up on people and...ow! Something sharp just pricked my hand!

SKINWALKER

The skinwalker is another creature who lived in the Americas long before Europeans came here. The Navajo people first recorded their existence hundreds and hundreds of years ago. The Navajo knew to stay away from skinwalkers. Anyone who doesn't listen to their wisdom is likely to end up dead...or worse.

Even talking about skinwalkers is forbidden among the Navajo and other native peoples. They know that if you mention them, if you talk about them...you might just call them to you.

Nobody wants that.

Skinwalkers were once people, but they used magic involving human sacrifice to gain the power of shapeshifting. They can change into any animal they choose. More than that, they can take over the mind of an animal and make it do whatever they choose. Usually what they choose is something very bad.

That's probably why, after spending a day in a small town in Nevada asking if anyone knew anything about skinwalkers, I found myself surrounded by angry coyotes. Their teeth were bared. Their eyes were red. They were all growling and snarling at me as if they were looking at their dinner.

The legend says that a bullet coated with white ash can kill a skin-walker and the animal they're controlling.

Luckily, I came prepared. But I'm down to my last bullet.

CACTUS CAT

The cactus cats roam across the deserts of the American southwest and northern Mexico. Just like the name implies, these monsters look like cats crossed with cactus plants. They have green thorns instead of fur, with especially long and spikey thorns on the ends of their ears and tail. Their tails even split, like the branches of a cactus plant. If one of them was sitting very still on the sands of the desert, you might think it was a cactus!

This is one of those monsters who won't cause you any trouble, as long as you leave it alone. I always do my best not to bother them when I'm in the desert. If I see anything that looks like a cactus just sitting there in the sun, I leave it alone. They do the same for me. I don't think they're afraid of me. I just think they know I'm not a threat.

Cactus cats don't usually attack people. They prefer to drink the sap of a cactus plant, and this could be how they got their unusual look. They use the spikes on their legs to cut the plants open so the sap will flow, and they can drink it. The sap, however, has the same effect on them that catnip has on ordinary cats, and makes them a little crazy. Whenever you hear a howling, screechy singing in the air at night in the desert, that's the cactus cats, getting frisky on cactus sap.

OLE HIGUE

This monster is a female vampire from the Caribbean, a group of islands in the Atlantic Ocean, just off the Gulf of Mexico. When you're looking for this monster, forget everything you thought you knew about vampires.

Ole Higue can go out in the daylight. It doesn't hurt her, and it doesn't kill her. The sunrise is no protection from this vampire.

During the day, she walks through the streets of various towns, looking like any other old woman. Nighttime is when she looks to feed. When the sun goes down, she peels off her skin and hides it in a gourd. Then...she catches fire!

As this ball of flame, she floats from place to place until she comes to her victim's house. When she finds one she likes, she shrinks herself down until she is just a tiny spark, big enough to fit through a keyhole, a crack or other small space. Worst of all, she prefers to feed on small children.

When I travel to the Caribbean, I know a few ways to protect myself from Ole Higue. One is to leave a key in the lock, to block her from coming in through the keyhole. Another is to leave a line of dry rice around whatever house you're staying in. When Ole Higue reaches a line of spilled rice, she can't help but count every single grain until she knows how many there are. If you put it in a circle, she won't remember where she started, and will simply keep counting all the way around, over and over, until the sun comes up and she has to put her skin back on!

SOUTH AMERICA

MADRE DE AGUAS

Cuba is an island country in the Gulf of Mexico. In the lakes and rivers of Cuba lives a monster called Madre de Aguas, which means "Mother of Waters." Although her name sounds beautiful, the monster is anything but.

Madre de Aguas is a huge snake, as big and as wide as a giant tree. On her head are two horns and her scales are as big as shields. They are tough and thick, and protect her from swords and knives, and even bullets.

This monster controls the waters in Cuba, from the flow of the rivers to the level of water in lakes. If someone digs a well for drinking water, they might connect to the waters that are controlled by Madre de Aguas. When the giant snake is fed and happy, the water levels are high, and there is plenty for everyone. But when she is angry, she will cause accidents and droughts.

Madre de Aguas is so large, she can even swallow up all the water. When I travel to Cuba, I always bring my own bottled water. I don't want to be drinking water that's been swallowed and spit out again by a monster like this.

ZOMBIE

Is there anything scarier than a human who won't stay dead? Imagine someone being buried, but then clawing their way out of their coffin and digging through the dirt to rise again in a mindless search to feed on human flesh...

The thing to remember about zombies is that they aren't all slow like you see in the movies. Some of them move as quick as you or I do. Zombies are like a disease. They carry the virus in them, so if they bite you, you will die and then turn into one of them. You will wake up trapped in a rotting corpse, craving human flesh, and will begin feeding on other people as you try to fill the bottomless hunger of death.

It's a little unclear where zombies originally came from. Everyone agrees they started in Haiti, but how they were created is a mystery. The believers of Voodoo were said to be able to use dark magic to raise the dead and make them slaves. The zombie slave would continue to rot and decay, but they would work for the Voodoo magician for as long as their bodies could still move.

This is what's known as a fate worse than death.

Apparently, the magic got away from the people using it, and the zombies started making more zombies as they fed on human flesh. And because zombies are already dead, they were nearly impossible to stop.

To kill a zombie, you must damage their brain. You can cut off their head or shoot them in the head. Either one works.

Just don't miss.

CHUPACABRA

Speaking of monsters who eat farm animals, there is a creature in South America called a chupacabra. It originally came from Puerto Rico. It was first seen there in the 1970s and now roams across South America and Mexico, and even the southern parts of the United States to drink the blood of animals like sheep and goats.

In fact, "chupacabra" means "goat sucker" in Spanish. Even though their main meal is animal blood, they will attack humans when cornered. They look like werewolves, with hairy bodies and big sharp teeth and they tend to attack anything that comes too close. That will include me, if I'm not careful.

After sneaking around animal herds in Mexico for days, I finally spotted the chupacabra one night as it snatched a sheep and bit the poor animal's neck. As it drank the blood, I took out my camera to take the pictures that would prove this monster was real. The flash went off, and the monster's long, hairy face turned toward me. Its glowing red eyes, illuminated by the flash, were staring right at me.

I've never been so happy not to be a goat!

TATA DUENDE

Belize is a small country in South America, just below Mexico. In the jungles of that hot place lives a demon by the name of Tata Duende, which translates to 'Grandfather Goblin.' He is an old, old creature, as old as the jungles themselves. With wrinkled skin, and a wide floppy hat, he stands only a few feet tall. At first you might mistake him for any old man you might meet on your travels, but then you notice he has no thumbs, and his feet are on backwards!

Tata Duende is hard to find. He creeps through the shadows of Belize's jungles in order to protect the birds and the animals. He makes sure that hunters never take more than they need to feed their families. If you're shooting animals for fun, Tata Duende will come hunting for you. If you're walking through the trees, you might see a little shadow following you, keeping a close eye on everything you do.

Sometimes Tata Duende gets bored, and ventures into nearby towns and villages to play tricks. He may not have any thumbs but he is very good at braiding hair. Farmers find braids in their horses' manes, and mothers find their little girls have had their hair braided into such complicated knots that they never come out.

If you let Tata Duende see you in the jungles, and if you aren't hunting his beloved animals, he might invite you to join him in his cave. There he'll feed you stew, and play his guitar for you with his four-fingered hands.

I've been invited myself, and he does play beautifully. I was very careful not to let him see my thumbs, though. Since he doesn't have any of his own, he's very jealous of anyone who has them. Sometimes, he becomes angry about it, and bites off the thumbs of his guests.

EL CADEJOS

This is a dog-like demon who prowls the roads of Costa Rica, a country in Central America. Some are all black and some are all white, but all of them are scary. They are huge creatures, with shaggy fur and blazing red eyes. Instead of paws, their feet are hooves, like a goat. There are chains around their necks because many people and other demons have tried to catch the cadejos, but they break free every time. You can hear the chains dragging on the ground wherever these monsters go.

Thankfully, the cadejos only come out at night. When they do, they jump on people and hold them down. They lick the person, because the cadejos can taste if you're a good person or not. If you're a good person, they will only lick you all over and then let you go, slobbering wet and scared to death.

But if you're a bad person, they'll eat you up.

I'm not worried, because I'm a good person. At least, I think I'm a good person. Maybe I should try to do more good deeds for my friends and family...

MUKI

The tallest mountain range in the Western Hemisphere are the Andes Mountains in South America. They reach from the southernmost tip of South America all the way up the West Coast, nearly to the top of that continent. The mountains tower over the lands below, casting them in shadows, and giving shelter to the deep forests of the area.

Another thing the mountains have in abundance are precious metals—gold, silver, and others that are worth a lot of money, if you can dig them out without getting yourself lost or hurt in the process. A creature called a muki lives in the mines of this area, and he knows the best ways to coax the precious metals out of the ground. He's a tiny elf-like creature who dresses in mining gear, complete with a yellow safety helmet with a light on top. He might be small, but he's stronger than any man, and his feet are very large, which gives him a strange, duck-like waddle when he walks.

Legend says that if you bring the muki his favorite treat—cocoa leaves—he'll buy them from you for gold and silver, or jewels. The only thing he asks in exchange is that you never talk about him. Don't tell anyone where your good fortune came from, just enjoy the riches he gives you in exchange for the sweet, delicious cocoa leaves.

What's that? Well, yes, I am talking about the muki. It's okay, though. I've already gotten enough gold from him. I'm going to the bank, and I'm never, ever setting foot in that mine again!

TEHU JAGUA

Tehu Jagua is a famous monster from Paraguay, a country in South America. It lives in its own little area, where the streets are covered in gold and gemstones. Tehu Jagua loves to roll around in all that wealth until its own skin shines like gold. The monster is said to be very kind to people, but it is also very stingy and selfish. All those riches, and it keeps them for itself.

Not many people have seen Tehu Jagua, or else they would be able to follow it back to where it lives and take some of that gold for themselves. Because it isn't seen very often, people disagree about what it looks like. When you do see it, most often all you see is a flash of gold in the distance as it disappears into the trees. Most agree it has the body of a giant lizard and a dog's head. Some even say it has seven heads, each of them barking like dogs. Whoever its mother was, it is supposed to be one of seven brothers, but the ugliest of all seven!

Thankfully, Tehu Jagua is a vegetarian. It doesn't eat people. It's known as the protector of the fruit trees all throughout Paraguay. So I figure the best way to trick the monster into showing itself so I can follow it back to its home of gold and jewels is to put out a big pile of fruit. Mangos, bananas, and ripe apples. I sit shrouded among the trees as I watch, and wait...

Until I hear the dogs barking behind me, and I take off running. Tehu Jagua may be a vegetarian, but I don't want to find out what it feels like to be bitten by seven dog heads all at once!

SACI-PERERÊ

Saci-Pererê is a wind spirit from the South American country of Brazil, where they speak Portuguese, a language similar to Spanish but also quite different.

This spirit controls all of Brazil's winds and even travels around on his own personal tornado. Probably for the best, considering he only has one leg. Hopping everywhere would take too long. He wears a magic red hat that allows him to be invisible whenever he wants, just like the wind. The magic of the hat only makes Saci-Pererê disappear, however. The hat itself doesn't disappear and this is how you know Saci-Pererê is around. Whenever you see a red hat floating through the air as if it's floating on the wind, you know the wind spirit is nearby.

Thankfully, this monster isn't evil. He doesn't do mean things to people or eat them...but he does like to play tricks. Sometimes he will ask people for a gift, but if they refuse to give him one, he might just play a trick on them. With Saci-Pererê, it's always Halloween!

Because he controls the winds, when he plays tricks he'll do things like steal cows and horses by lifting them up, up, and away. Or he'll push plates and glasses off the table to break them. Some stories say he can put a curse on your eggs so you can never break them open to have breakfast.

According to the stories in Brazil, if you can catch Saci-Pererê, he'll grant you a wish to get you to let him go. No one has ever been able to catch him, though, because he's as fast as the wind. I'm not worried about that. I've come prepared. I bet no one has ever tried to suck him up in a vacuum cleaner before!

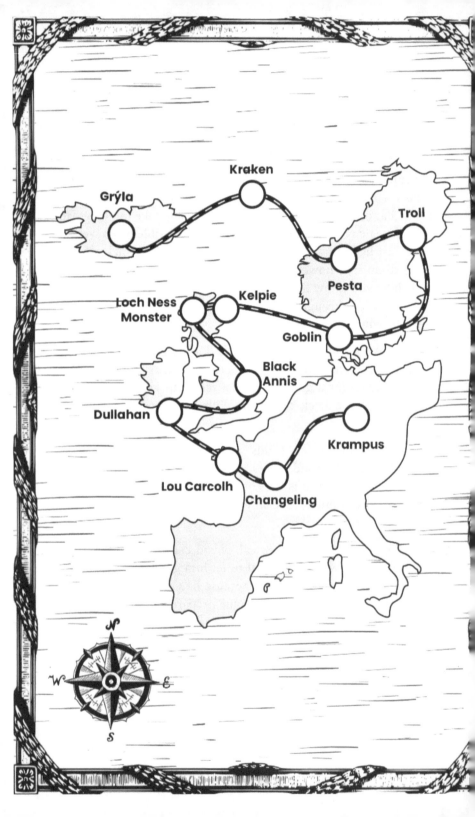

WESTERN EUROPE

THE GRÝLA

Iceland is a country far to the north, up near the Arctic Circle. Because of how far north it is, in the winter months, daylight in Iceland only lasts for a few hours and the rest of the day is shrouded in darkness. Elves and trolls are said to roam the chilly, dark landscape during these times of darkness, but the scariest creature one might encounter during this time is by far the Grýla.

The Grýla is also known as the Christmas Witch. She's so old that there are stories about her from seven hundred years ago. Some claim she is nothing more than a giant or a troll, but the truth is that she is much more than that. She is big and hairy, but she also has a tail. Oh, and I should tell you about the bag on her neck.

She uses the bag to carry away naughty children from their families. Even worse, she likes to cook these children in her stew pot. For her, this is a yearly tradition.

This monster has thirteen ears on each side of her head so she can hear everything the children in the village below are doing while she sits in front of the fire in her home high up in the mountains. She hears when they're being bad. I've tried to warn the children of Iceland to be good, but sometimes they merely laugh at me. The Christmas Witch can't be real, they say, refusing to believe me.

Maybe they'll believe me after Christmas, when some of their friends are missing. I'm going to stay up all night trying to make sure that doesn't happen, but that witch is very, very hungry.

THE KRAKEN

The Kraken is a huge and very old sea monster that lives in the ocean waters of northern Europe. It is the largest squid ever, with long and huge tentacles that can wrap around ships and pull them under the water. Many believe it is over a mile long. That's more than fifty blue whales set end to end, and they're the largest animal to have ever existed on Earth!

Of course, the Kraken feeds on the sailors of the boats it sinks. Being that big, I imagine all the fish in the sea aren't enough to satisfy its appetite. No wonder it feeds on people, too. I'm not saying I agree with it, just that I understand it.

The good thing about the Kraken is that it can't get very close to shore because it's so large. It has to stay in deep water. You'll be safe if you just swim in the rivers and lakes near you. If you do decide to go out in the deep water, just keep an eye out for gigantic tentacles heading your way.

PESTA

In the twelfth century, Europe was devastated by one of the worst plagues the world has ever known. This outbreak of bubonic plague was known as the "Black Death" because so many people died from the disease. It gradually spread across the globe, leaving death and grief in its wake, but the worst of the plague happened in Europe.

Norway was one of the countries most affected. More than half of the population died during the plague. When it was over, entire towns were left empty. No family had gone untouched by the Black Death. The burials of the dead never seemed to stop.

It was believed that the Black Death was spread throughout Norway by a witch with a face as pale as ash. The witch had been wronged by the man she loved, and so in retribution for his cruel acts, she spread the plague to his family, and his friends, and then continued to bring death wherever she went.

The witch's true name has been lost to history, but at some point she took the name Pesta, and that was what everyone called her. "Pesta" is Norwegian for plague, or pestilence.

The stories say that Pesta traveled across Norway, going from town to town with a rake and a broom, using one or the other each time she arrived. If she raked the ground, it meant the people in the town would live. If she used the broom to sweep the ground, however, it meant everyone living there would soon perish.

No one knows what happened to Pesta. Perhaps she got her fill of revenge and stopped. Maybe she came to the last town in Norway and had nowhere else to go. Or perhaps the Black Death killed even her. Thankfully, with the advances in medicine that modern times have brought us, the bubonic plague is no longer a danger, so Pesta would not be able to use it to cast her revenge anyway.

But just in case, it's always a good rule to be nice to people.

TROLL

Trolls are monsters whose origins are in Scandinavia, which is comprised of Norway, Denmark, and Sweden. Trolls have been around for a very long time and there are many stories about them. Different countries have added their own stories, but the original stories are still the scariest.

In the first stories about trolls, they were described as big, hairy giants who lived in castles that were sometimes built under mountains. They left their homes only after dark because sunlight could hurt them. If they didn't return to their castles before dawn, the sun would turn them to stone.

In fact, that is said to have happened many, many times. Some of the mountains in Scandinavia are said to have been formed by trolls who weren't smart enough to escape the sun. They were turned to stone, and over time, dirt and rocks and other things collected on them, which created tall mountains that still exist today.

I've often wondered what would happen if someone dug deep enough in those mountains. Would they find the troll, still there in the form of a stone statue?

Digging down into stone isn't easy, so maybe no one will ever know. The few times I tried, I only found gold and silver. No trolls. At least, not that I know of. There were some very interesting rocks that I couldn't identify, though. I've kept them in my collection and maybe someday their origins will be revealed to me.

People who wanted to walk around at night safe from the trolls had just one defense. As it happens, trolls have very sensitive hearing. A ringing bell would hurt their ears and send them running, and screaming for mercy. Many towns had a bell that would ring at night, to keep the people safe. Hopefully, the ringtone on my cell phone will have the same effect, since I'm walking around right now after dark.

GOBLIN

Goblins are small, ugly creature, shorter than a person, with skin that is a pale green or sickly yellow color. Their teeth are yellow and crooked, and very sharp. Although goblins like to hurt people, and do very mean things to them, they do not usually eat people. But that doesn't mean they never do, so it's best not to take chances. If you see a goblin, you should run. They're fast, though, so your best bet is to try not to meet a goblin.

That doesn't mean the goblin won't try to meet you. Goblins live to create mischief. They will sneak into people's homes to break things, or spray paint pictures on the wall, or eat half the food in the refrigerator and leave the refrigerator door open so the rest of the food will spoil. Sometimes they will even creep into your home while you're asleep, carrying a big ball of bad dreams they have woven out of cobwebs. They will tiptoe up to your bed and feed the nightmares into your ear so that all night long your dreams will be ruined.

If you've ever read *The Lord of the Rings,* then you know as much about goblins as most people do. You don't need special tools or magic to take care of a goblin. They're one of the few truly flesh and blood monsters. They're just nastier and meaner than regular people like you and me.

Goblins usually live in caves, or underground, but they like to live near towns and houses. Have you checked around your house for holes? Or caves?

KELPIE

In the highlands of Scotland, among the lush fields and crystal-blue rivers, lives a monster of a different sort. An evil fairy creature that appears as a horse but can change its shape into a pretty human—either a boy or a girl—to lure people to it by promising love.

Luckily, even shapeshifters like these make mistakes now and then. If you look at the hair of a kelpie, you'll find sand from the shores of the water where they live, and seaweed as well. Of course, if you get close enough to comb a kelpie's hair, then you're too close. That's when they grab you, return to their horse form, and try to drag you into the water. They can breathe underwater, too.

I can't breathe underwater. Can you?

There is one weakness that all kelpie have, though. Because they are fairy creatures, they can be controlled with the right kind of magic. If you can find one, there is a magic bridle that was created before recorded history, back when horses ran free and wild across most of the Earth. Back then, kelpies could hide themselves more easily. Some of you may know that a bridle is a connected set of straps that go around a horse's head and in their mouth. The bridle and the reins allow you to direct a horse's movements.

No wild horse would ever allow a bridle to be put on them. Kelpies fight hard when you try to put a bridle on them. They fight and fight, and all the while they drag you toward the water, hoping to drown you before you can control them...

THE LOCH NESS MONSTER

The Loch Ness Monster is one of the most famous monsters in the world. Affectionately nicknamed "Nessie" by many, it lives in the Scottish lake of Loch Ness. It looks like a dinosaur, similar to the brontosaurus. It is huge, and grayish, with a long bendy neck. In fact, some people believe it may be a dinosaur left over from when they roamed the Earth.

There have been some photos taken of Nessie, but just like with other monster photographs, these were not very good quality, and left doubt about what the photographers actually saw. Researchers have searched the entire length of Loch Ness, from one end to the other, and haven't found a trace of any monsters living there.

That's because, big as she is, Nessie is very good at playing hide and seek. She can float down to the bottom of the lake and cover herself with sand, making her impossible to see unless she wants to be seen. She can also hide behind huge rock outcroppings at the bottom of the lake. It's hard to say where Nessie will be hiding when you go look for her. If you're very lucky, she might be feeling extra silly that day, and let you take another blurry picture of her. I've got half a dozen of them. In one of them, I swear she's smiling.

BLACK ANNIS

Black Annis was a very mean witch who lived in the county of Leicestershire in England back in the 18th and 19th centuries. She was tall and thin, with claws of iron instead of fingernails. Her skin was so pale it was almost blue. Her eyes glowed brightly in the dark. She wore clothing made from the skin of the people she had killed. She would sew them together and wear them like leather.

Black Annis would prowl the villages of Leicestershire and reach through the windows of people's houses to try to snatch away the children who were playing or sleeping inside. Parents would walk into their children's rooms to check on them, only to find them gone.

She lived in the hills, in a cave she'd carved herself with her iron claws. Near the cave's entrance was a huge oak tree and she would sometimes hide in the oak's shadow and wait for people to pass by. If anyone was foolish enough to venture that close to her cave, she would jump on them and devour them down to their bones.

The only way to stop the witch was to trap her in her own cave. The people of the village waited for her to be asleep and then they piled dirt, stones, tree branches and whatever else they could find over the cave's opening. She was sealed up, and even her magic couldn't get her out. They could hear her screams for days, until one day they stopped. Everyone assumed she'd died.

Now, after weeks of searching, I've finally found her cave. It's still sealed up after all these years. Holding a shovel, I'm wondering... should I look to see if she's really dead? Maybe she's just been quiet all these years, waiting for someone like me to set her free.

DULLAHAN

Ireland is home to leprechauns, and fairies, and all sorts of gentle magical creatures. But there are darker things that walk along the grass-covered hills and forests, as well. One of these is a headless ghost called a Dullahan, which in Celtic simply means "Headless Man."

That's not to say that the Dullahan is without a head. He carries it under his arm as he rides a horse across the land, seeking out unsuspecting travelers. He rides in the dark, after sunset, usually on days during a festival.

On a moonlit night during an Irish festival, I walked through the streets of a quaint little town nestled on the shores of Loch Narwin. There had been reports of this monster riding his big dark horse there for the past few days, and I wanted to see it. Everyone in the town shuttered their windows at night and stayed in bed, but I was determined to prove this monster was real.

Shortly after midnight I heard the sound of thundering hooves and saw the horse coming, tromping the ground so hard that sparks rose from the cobblestone street. He let out a ghostly wail as he raised his head up high, holding it by hair that had long since turned gray.

It is said that if the Dullahan speaks your name on one of his rides, then you are destined to die that very night.

Do you know what my name is? The Dullahan does.

LOU CARCOLH

This monster is a creature that comes from a region of France called Les Landes. As monsters go, this one is pretty gross.

The Lou Carcolh is a giant snail-like serpent, bigger than a house. The squishy body underneath its massive shell has hundreds of long, wriggling tentacles sprouting from it. Just like the tiny snails it resembles, this creature leaves slime wherever it goes.

Lou Carcolh lives in a cave under a town in Les Landes, and when it's hungry, it simply crawls along the ground, wandering aimlessly, leaving its slime trails everywhere. The people who live nearby must be careful to avoid these trails, because if they step in them, they'll be stuck.

If they can't free themselves in time, Lou Carcolh will find them and yank them up with its tentacles, then drag them back to its cave. There it feasts, devouring the poor, helpless human in the same way it does everything—very, very slowly.

Because it is so slow, the easiest thing to do, of course, is to run away as soon as you see it. Just watch out for the slime trails as you're running. As I just found out, it's very hard to run if both of your feet are stuck in slime.

CHANGELING

There are many, many different kinds of fairies who live in Europe. Some are nice, and they'll lend you a hand if you give them a gift first. Some of them want to avoid human contact altogether, so they're hard to find and rarely seen.

Other fairies, however, are mean. Some of them are pure evil.

The changeling is a monster that makes itself look like a mother's own baby. If the fairy folk find a baby that they think is particularly beautiful, they'll steal the human baby and leave the changeling in its place. The changeling will look exactly like the baby who was stolen. So much so that the mother doesn't even know the switch was made! She'll love the changeling baby as her own. She'll feed it, and change it, and read it stories.

It takes a long time, but eventually the parents will notice the difference because the changeling baby doesn't grow out of infancy. It can only take the one form, and can't change after that. The changeling is NOT a baby, though. Sometimes, parents might catch a glimpse of their baby playing an instrument, or dancing. That's a sure tip-off that the baby isn't human.

That's why I'm here, in this hospital's maternity ward. I'm on the trail of a changeling, trying to help a mother who thinks she's been tricked by the fairies. If we can find the changeling, and force it to turn back to its fairy form, the fairies will return the real baby.

Personally, I think it's the baby in the corner bassinet, smoking a cigar.

KRAMPUS

Christmas is supposed to be a time of joy and giving presents to the people you love. A time of light and happiness. A time when Santa leaves gifts for the boys and girls who have made his "Nice" list that year.

But some monsters bring only darkness. Krampus comes visiting in December just like Santa Claus does, but for very different reasons. He's looking for the kids who have been naughty. Not to give them gifts, either. Krampus grabs the naughty boys and girls, and carts them off in a washtub that he carries on his back.

Krampus is easy enough to spot, and I am looking for him right now. I don't want him to steal any more kids this year. Naughty or not, no kid deserves that. This monster is a tall, half-man, half-goat, with giant curved horns on the sides of his head. His feet are hooves. He has shaggy hair all over his body. Around his neck he wears dangling chains that clink and rattle, which he uses to tie up the children he steals.

You'd think it would be easy enough to find a monster like that, right? The thing is, every December the towns in Germany celebrate Krampus with a special parade called the "Krampuslauf," which is German for the Krampus Run. People dress up like Krampus and dance through the streets playing drums and carrying washtubs on their backs.

Now here I am, standing on the side of the road in the crowd, wondering which one of these Krampuses in the parade is the real one. Most of them are fakes, but I know the real monster is in there somewhere. If I can't find him, there will be more children stolen out of their beds this Christmas.

I sure hope you've been good this year. If you haven't, you might want to stay awake on Christmas night.

EASTERN EUROPE

GOLEM

This creature originally comes from Jerusalem in the Middle East, but became most famous in eastern Europe. It is created with a little bit of magic, and a little bit of faith, and a whole lot of clay.

The golem is created by someone who knows how to mold clay in a specific way, shaping a large man with big arms and legs and sometimes shoulders that go up to the top of the monster's bald head. Then comes the magic part. The golem is crafted with an open mouth, and whoever is in control of the monster will put instructions for it on a piece of paper, and put the paper in its mouth.

The golem must do whatever is written on the paper, no matter what it says. Jewish leaders would use the golem to protect towns and villages from anyone who would try to harm them. Rumor says there were several golems fighting for the Jewish people against the Nazis during World War II.

The problem is that the golem must do whatever is on the paper that is put into its mouth. So when the wrong person controls it, it can be made to do bad things, like rob people and damage property, and no one can stop it because it isn't really alive. It's hardened clay, or basically stone, with no mind of its own.

So, at the moment, I'm trying to stop this golem from rampaging through the village and destroying everyone's homes. All I have to do is grab the paper out of its mouth and replace it with another one that says "protect." I just need to reach my hand into that stone mouth, and hope it doesn't bite down when I do...

DYBBUK

Some monsters are flesh and blood. Some are ghosts. Often, it's hard to tell which one is scarier.

The dybbuk terrorizes people in Eastern Europe. People who did bad things in life, like rob people or hurt others for fun, were cursed so their spirits would wander forever instead of being at peace. They were evil in life, and now they're mad and desperate in death.

If you ever needed a reason to be good to people while you're alive, just remember, if you're not, you might become a dybbuk.

People cursed to be dybbuk ghosts want their body back. They want to be alive again. Since they can't have their own, they'll take anyone else's they can get ahold of. They inhabit a person like a hermit crab crawls into a new shell. The person they're in is helpless to do anything to force them out. They can only watch as the dybbuk takes up its old ways, using their body to do terrible, mean things to everyone around them.

Walking the streets of Eastern Europe, like I'm doing tonight, isn't always smart. Then again, when you're a monster hunter, you have to go where the monsters are. You have to risk your life—and your body—to see the worst things in the world.

The only cure for being inhabited by a dybbuk is an exorcism performed by a rabbi, the religious leaders of the Jewish faith.

If we meet someday, and I say something mean to you...please save me from the dybbuk.

Please?

VODYANOY

These monsters are nasty water creatures from the Czech Republic and Slovakia. They were first discovered in the lakes and waters of that part of Europe back in the 1800s, but they have lived there for much, much longer than that.

These creatures are as tall as a human. They have scaly fish tails and the head of a frog, but the body and arms of a human. Their burning red eyes blaze through the dark waters. Their hair is rough and green like moss. They're ugly and they're mean.

Their favorite thing to do is to drown people and animals. If they can grab you while you're swimming, they'll drag you underwater and try to keep you there until you run out of air. If there is no one swimming, they'll try to lure people into the water by leaving shiny objects on the riverbank, like jewels or small mirrors. When the unsuspecting person comes down to the water's edge to see what treasure they've found, the vodyanoy grab them and pull them under.

If the vodyanoy can't find enough victims to drown, they get angry. When they get angry, they break dams and wash out lumber mills. To appease this monster, fishermen, loggers, and even beekeepers will make sacrifices to keep them happy. That's why I always carry a jar of honey with me. If I see a pile of shiny jewels on the river's edge, I throw the jar into the water first. That way, I can walk off with the jewels before the vodyanoy even knows I was there.

BABA YAGA

Witches exist in every country in the world. Some of them are nice, some are not. I've met more than a few of them myself and I'm getting pretty good at telling the good from the bad. Baba Yaga was one of the scariest witches I've ever seen.

This witch lives in Russia, and she's been alive for several hundred years. Maybe that's why she looks like a thin, wrinkled old woman with scraggly white hair. Or maybe that's just the way she wants to appear to people. She has very strong magical powers. She can even fly through the sky in a huge mortar and pestle, tools used for grinding spices into powder for medicine or cooking...or secret witchcraft spells.

It wasn't hard for me to find Baba Yaga. She lives in the forests of the darkest parts of Russia, but her house is easy to spot. It's never in the same place twice. It walks through the woods—on tall chicken legs! It's true. All I had to do was follow the big bird tracks until I found her house, right there in front of me, staring down at me from high above.

I was taking a risk looking for her. When Baba Yaga is hungry, she eats people. She grinds them up in her mortar and pestle and then puts them in a stew. If she's not hungry, though, and if she's in a good mood, she might just help you out with a magic spell or two. I'm still here, so as you can see, it worked out for me. Baba Yaga must have been in a good mood that day.

Although, every now and then I do still cluck like a chicken.

ZMEI GORYNYCH

This monster has its origins in Russian folklore. It was a winged dragon with three heads and huge, copper claws. It was so huge that when it flew through the sky, it blotted out the sun and made the whole world go dark.

Zmei Gorynych lived in the forests and mountains of Russia. Its name means "Snake of the Mountains." It would fly around and swoop down upon unsuspecting villages and towns and snatch people right off their feet. It would eat them, and then come back for more. It would burn crops for fun. If there were no people to steal, it would take the sheep and cows in the fields, and the people would go hungry.

Unlike most other dragons, Zmei Gorynych could talk. It could also change its shape to be something else, or to become very small. When brave people would try to kill it, the dragon would make itself teeny tiny and beg for mercy. Sometimes, this trick worked. Other times, the heroes in the stories recognized the trick for what it was.

Big or small, Zmei Gorynych was still evil. Eventually a hero killed the dragon, so it no longer stalks the Russian people.

That's good. There are plenty of other monsters in the world, so one less monster is a relief.

BALAUR

The balaur is a dragon that comes from Romania, an Eastern European country shrouded in mystery. It is a huge green reptile, with long leathery wings, a long tail and long neck, and sharp claws on its scaly feet. Its reptilian snout is full of big, sharp fangs. Oh, and of course, since it's a dragon, it naturally breathes fire.

Once upon a time, this monster was a snake like any other snake. According to the tales about the balaur, the snake became trapped underground for twelve years, so it wasn't able to bite anything in all that time. It turns out if a snake isn't able to bite things, it begins to grow bigger and bigger. It will grow legs and wings, and eventually will become a dragon. When that happens, it becomes strong enough to break out of the ground, and when it's out it's very angry about what was done to it.

As a result, the balaur will kidnap people and devour them. It will use its wings to cause terrible storms that do damage to Romania's towns, scattering animal herds and destroying crops.

The oldest and angriest of the balaur grow extra necks and heads. The most heads ever recorded on a balaur was twelve, one head for each year it was trapped underground. Because each of the heads can breathe fire, a balaur of that type is an extremely dangerous monster.

Some people say you need to have a strong sword to kill a dragon. I think I'm going to start with a fire extinguisher instead.

VAMPIRE

Vampires are the most famous of all monsters. I knew I had to meet one, and I knew just where to look.

As I'm sure you know, vampires are the undead. They aren't alive, not like you and me, but they aren't exactly dead, either. They are something in between. Something...unholy. They sleep in their coffins by day and only come out at night, so if you want to see one, you have to go where the coffins are. Which is why I'm in a graveyard at the stroke of midnight.

Luckily, vampires have certain weaknesses. They avoid the daylight because sunlight will kill them. Garlic will repel them. Holy water, blessed by the Church, will burn them. A wooden stake driven through their heart will turn them to dust—if you can get close enough to try!

Vampires feed on human blood. Their evil power increases when they have drained a victim of all the blood in their veins. At their strongest, vampires can control your mind and make you do things you don't want to do. They can move faster than your eyes can see. In the book *Dracula,* by Bram Stoker, we learn that vampires can turn into bats and fly away.

Tonight, I'm walking through this cemetery to find a blood-sucking vampire. The gravestones stand tall in the night, casting terrifying dark shadows everywhere. When I find the grave I'm looking for, the one where a vampire sleeps, I find the coffin standing open...and empty.

Above me, I hear a squeak, and in the moonlight I can just make out a bat flying away.

THE ÖRDÖG

The Ördög is a very old and very nasty demon from Hungary, a country in Central Europe. Although he likes to spend time in the beautiful forests of that country, the demon's home is actually in Hell, where all demons live. While he's in Hell, he stirs a giant cauldron full of human souls over a burning fire. Every once in a while, he'll taste the souls as if he's tasting a delicious soup, so he can decide if they've stewed long enough.

This monster can shapeshift into different people and animals. This is how he's able to hide in plain sight as he searches for victims and takes notes about who might end up in Hell when they die. Be careful what you do in public. Be careful what you say. You never know when the Ördög will be listening.

When he isn't hiding in someone else's shape or as a friendly pet, he looks like a man from the waist up, with the hairy legs and stubby tail of a goat. Above his pointy ears are large curling horns. Now it's easy to see why the demon hides in the shape of other things.

The Ördög will travel the forests it loves disguised as a shepherd. If he meets someone, he'll try to make a bet with them. Something like: guess how many toadstools are under a rotting log, or how many eggs are in a bird's nest. If this ever happens to you, don't take the bet! If you lose, your soul will be sent straight to Hell to end up in the Ördög's cauldron.

Don't say I didn't warn you.

CYCLOPS

This big guy is a monster from Greek mythology. He has a human body of massive proportions, is dozens and dozens of feet tall, and has huge muscles. Except he has only one eye instead of two, and he has a big horn curling up from the middle of his forehead. He was a Titan, a race of beings who fought against the god Zeus for control of Mount Olympus. The Titans lost, but they still hung around, and were mighty angry about being banished from their heavenly home.

Even with just one eye, the cyclops was said to be a great craftsman. Supposedly, he built many of Greece's greatest buildings. In spite of that, he was not a good monster. He fed on humans, and it took a lot of regular-sized Greek people to fill him up!

There were actually three cyclops; brothers named Arges, Steropes, and Brontes. Although the Greek heroes of myth killed one or two of them over the years, at least one of them is still wandering about, building things and looking for its next meal of human flesh. I personally haven't seen one, but I'm not complaining.

THE MINOTAUR

The Minotaur is a frightening creature from Greek mythology. That means you aren't likely to run into it today, which is a good thing. With the body of a man and the head of a bull, it was tall and strong and very, very angry.

A lot of strange things happened in Greek mythology. In the Minotaur's case, it had a human mother, Queen Pasiphae, who was the wife of King Minos. The Minotaur's father, however, was a white bull. When King Minos saw the child that Pasiphae had given birth to, he created an endless labyrinth to keep the Minotaur hidden away so no one could ever see it. "Labyrinth" is a fancy name for a very tricky maze full of traps and dangers. The only people sent into the labyrinth were people Minos wanted to punish. Those people were the only food the Minotaur had all year.

One year, a hero named Theseus asked to be sent into the labyrinth. Theseus was smart. He knew that not even the Minotaur could find his way out of that maze, so he brought a ball of string with him. As he walked, he let the string unravel behind him, so when he wanted to leave, he could follow the string and retrace his steps back to the door.

The Minotaur almost killed Theseus, but in the end Theseus won. He killed the beast so no one else would ever have to die in the labyrinth.

Some people say the Minotaur had children, however. There might still be hulking half-man, half-bull creatures out there, lurking in tunnels, or dark hallways, or anywhere that reminds them of their home—the labyrinth.

THE MIDDLE EAST & AFRICA

GRIFFIN

The griffin comes from ancient Egypt and Persia (the region now called Iran). He is perhaps the oldest monster in the world, more than five thousand years old, at least.

The griffin is a large creature with the body of a lion and the head and wings of an eagle. Because it's part bird, it lives in a huge nest that it makes itself with sticks and straw and mud. It even lays eggs like an eagle, except the eggs' shells are made of stone. It's a hard way for baby griffins to be born.

The griffin was sometimes thought to be a protector of the people of Egypt, or of specific places. It also guards the entrances of mines and places in the desert that hold buried treasure.

The griffin's claws are said to have great medicinal purposes. Ground up and used as a powder, the claws can heal many things. I'm not sure the griffin will want to part with its claw, but maybe it will let me trim its toenails, if I ask nicely?

DJINN

Djinn are paranormal creatures, spirits that grant wishes to those who enslave them. Of course, no one likes to be forced to serve anyone against their will, so the genies often harbor a grudge against their masters, and do whatever they can to make the wishes come out wrong. They are also very proud creatures and if they believe someone has done them wrong, they can curse that person with a terrible and painful disease.

There are several ways to spell this monster's name, depending on what language one is using. Genie. Djinn or Jinn. I've also seen it spelled Jinnee.

These monsters come straight out of Arabian myths. They tell us that genies existed long before humans did. When humanity began to populate the Earth in large numbers, magicians and sorcerers learned how to capture the genies by locking the spirit inside of an object. The most famous of these, of course, is the magic lamp of Aladdin. However, genies could be trapped in any household item, like a vase, or a rug. Once the genie is trapped, it has no choice but to grant wishes to the person who owns that item. Some stories say there's a limited number of wishes, while other stories say the number of wishes is unlimited.

Excuse me, please. I'm going to go check the things in my house to see if there's a genie trapped inside any of them. I could certainly use a few wishes!

This monster is known in its native land of Qatar, a country in the Middle East, as Homarat Al-Guyla. She is a part-woman, part-donkey creature, although no one is quite sure which parts are human and which parts are donkey. That's because, like many women in the Middle East, she wears a full body covering called a burka. It covers her from her ankles all the way up to the top of her head. Even her face is covered! This is a perfect way for her to hide among human women, and keep herself from being noticed.

The Homarat Al-Guyla is also known as the "Donkey of Noon" because that is when she wanders about, stalking her prey—little children. In hot and arid desert countries like Qatar, it is too hot at noontime for people to be outside. Most take a nap at midday. They don't want the children to run off on their own, or play in the hot sun where they could get sunburned and suffer heat stroke. The children know they're supposed to stay inside and only bad children ignore this rule and sneak outside.

It's these children the Donkey Lady looks for.

If she finds children wandering the streets at midday, she snatches them away, and they're never seen again. If she doesn't find any children outside, she will sometimes walk up to people's doors and knock. If a child opens the door, the Donkey Lady knows they weren't taking a nap like they were told to do, and she grabs them and takes them to her secret lair. No one knows what happens to them there, but they will never be seen again.

The only way to tell if it is the Donkey Lady walking up to your door rather than one of your friends or neighbors is to listen for the sound of her footsteps. She has hooves for feet, so she makes a clip-clop sound when she walks.

Listen for that sound, and if you hear it coming, you'd better be sure to jump under your covers and pretend to be asleep! Whatever you do, don't answer the door when your parents have told you to stay in your room and take a nap. Sometimes, your parents really do know best.

LAU

The lau is a monster who lives in the rivers of Sudan, one of the largest countries in the northeastern part of Africa. It looks very much like the huge aquatic dinosaurs called Plesiosaurs. It has a long, rounded body but instead of legs it has four massive flippers. Its tail is short and stubby. Its long neck supports a reptilian head full of sharp teeth. This monster also has lots and lots of tentacles writhing about its snout that it uses to catch and draw prey into its hungry mouth. The noise it makes is just like an elephant's, so if you decide to hunt the lau, you have to make sure you aren't just trailing some helpless pachyderm.

Just like many other monsters, the lau prefers to feast on humans. As a human myself, I would rather not end up as its lunch. That's why this beast needs to be hunted. If possible, to catch it, but if necessary...well, let's just hope it doesn't come to that.

People say the lau leaves a deep trail along the riverbank when it crawls onto land looking for people to catch and eat. It also burrows into the ground when it feels threatened. So, at the moment, I'm walking the paths along a river to see if I can find a trail dragged through the dirt. The holes they make when they do that must be massive.

Now that I've found a trail, I'll follow it until I find a hole. The problem with trails like this, however, is that you never know if it's going away from you...or coming toward you. I guess there's only one way to find out.

LUKWATA

In nearly every large body of water in the world, there lives a monster. They are usually huge and serpent-like. Lake Victoria in Africa is no exception. It is the largest lake in all of Africa, and the largest tropical lake in the world. In fact, the lake is so large that it sits in three different countries—Uganda, Kenya, and Tanzania.

There are many different stories about what the Lukwata looks like. The only way to know for sure is to find the beast, and take a picture of it. Even if I see it, no one will believe me without a picture. That's why most monsters are considered to be nothing more than myths. If they can't see it for themselves, people don't want to believe it.

Some people say the Lukwata looks like a giant serpent. Some say it looks like a giant fish. I'm pretty sure those people are only seeing part of it every time it appears. Because other people who have seen it say it is over a hundred feet long, with a long snake-like body that is humped like a fish, and a snake's head that is ringed by many, many tentacles.

In other words, truly terrifying.

With a monster like that in their lake, you might wonder why it hasn't eaten all the people for miles around. Well, I've found the answer. Apparently it's scared of crocodiles! There are hundreds of Nile crocodiles that live in Lake Victoria. They're scary all by themselves, but they keep the people safe from the Lukwata. I guess sometimes you need one monster to keep another away.

ETOKO

This monster lives in what is now the country of the Democratic Republic of Congo, but it existed long before it was called that. It lives in the rainforests, making a home inside hollow trees. While plenty of creatures live in the rainforests and don't bother anyone, the etoko is something different. It has a reason to hide as it waits for people to walk by.

Although small enough to hide in a tree, the etoko is very strong. The legends about this monster say that only heroes or magic users could ever fight it and win. It has a beard made of glass and clothes made of leaves. Tiny black eyes. A long snout instead of a nose. Sharp, sharp teeth. Its favorite meal? You guessed it. People.

The etoko doesn't go out to hunt people, however. It waits in its tree until someone walks by. Then it rings a special magic bell. If humans hear the bell, they fall under a spell and have no choice but to follow the sound right up to the tree where the etoko is living. That's when dinner is served.

So today I'm walking through the rainforests in the Democratic Republic of Congo, looking for a monster who lives in trees. Don't worry. He's not going to get me. I'm wearing noise-cancelling headphones. If he rings that bell, I won't hear it.

KIKIYAON

This super scary monster lives in Senegal, a country in Africa. It looks sort of like a giant owl, with its big round eyes, sharp beak, and massive wings. But instead of feathers on its body, it's covered in green hair. The kikiyaon has arms and legs like a human's, though, and a bird's talons for feet.

The kikiyaon smells like rotting meat, which can help warn you if it's coming up behind you in an attempt to snatch you off your feet and devour you. It also makes a loud grunting noise that can be heard from miles away when it's excited. This monster tends to be lazy, and will hide in hollow trees waiting for a victim to walk by so it can simply pounce on them instead of having to expend any effort to find its meal.

Remember to walk carefully through the woods when you're in Senegal. Hollow trees can be hiding lots of things. Biting insects. Poisonous snakes.

Or maybe a giant owl monster that wants to make you its next meal.

KHODUMODUMO

This monster stomps its way around the countryside of South Africa. The khodumodumo, or "swallowing monster" looks like a giant inflated lizard with a huge frog's mouth and eyes. It is hundreds of feet tall. It is so big, in fact, that it can only crawl its way along the ground. In its huge mouth are lots and lots of sharp tongues that are impossible to escape.

The khodumodumo crawls its way through the countryside, swallowing everything in its path. Trees. Rocks. Animals. And yes, people. It's a lot like a huge, living vacuum cleaner.

The thing is, the monster doesn't digest its victims immediately. They sit in its stomach for a long time, still alive. There is a story that the khodumodumo was so humongous that as it crawled its way along it got stuck between two mountains. It tried and tried to free itself, but it couldn't move forward or backward. But then along came a hero, who stabbed the monster in the belly. Out from the hole in its belly came every person and animal it had eaten. They were still alive, and were very happy to be free. As they piled out of the monster, it deflated like a balloon until it could wiggle its way out from between the mountains. The hero didn't kill it, but he did save all those people.

The khodumodumo is still out there, still dragging its way through South Africa. Just remember, if you're ever swallowed up by this monster, look for the hole in its side. You just might be able to escape.

THE GROOTSLANG

The Orange River is the largest river in South Africa. Wherever you have large rivers like this, you usually find large monsters. Spotting them is only a matter of sitting and waiting, watching carefully and hoping you see the monster before it sees you.

The Grootslang is forty feet long. That's longer than a school bus! Its eyes are actually large diamonds that sparkle and glitter in the sun. Although it has the body of a snake, it has the head of an elephant, with floppy ears and a long, bendy nose. It has tusks, and the fangs of a snake. It will often come up out of the water and use its long nose to grab cows that are drinking by the side of the river, then bite them with its fangs and spear them with its tusks, and drag them under the water to feed on them.

Now you know why I'm hiding and lying in wait to see this monster. I don't want to be its next meal.

The myth of how the Grootslang was created claims that their creator looked upon this monster and saw that it was too gruesome to exist, so it was split into two animals: the snake and the elephant. In other words, from this ugly monster came two very useful animals.

But some of the Grootslang escaped the change forced on them by their creator. A few of them continued to be what they are—monsters. These remaining Grootslang are said to live in a special cave near the Orange River, a cave called the bottomless pit. This cave is supposed to be full of diamonds. But those 'diamonds' might just be the eyes of the Grootslang, staring at you, waiting to spring.

It's believed that if you are attacked by one of these monsters, you can escape by throwing jewels at it. I've got two pouches of rubies and emeralds in my travel bag. I sure hope that's enough!

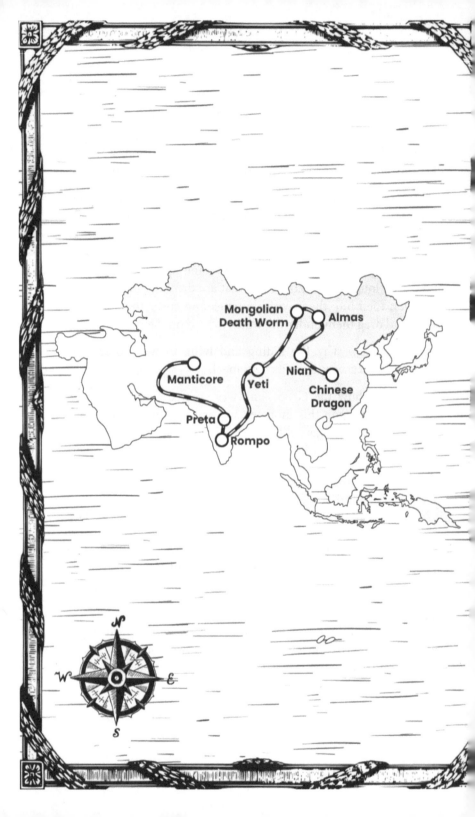

ASIA

MANTICORE

This monster is another creature that appears to be made from parts of other animals. With the face of a man and the body and mane of a lion, and the tail of a scorpion, this beast is nothing to fool with. It is sometimes called 'manticore' and sometimes called a 'man-tiger.' It has been around for centuries, and with very few natural predators, it's likely to be around for a very, very long time to come.

Many monsters formed a long time ago continue to live in today's world. In case you're wondering why, it's because monsters live forever. Just because you haven't seen one, doesn't mean they no longer exist.

The manticore was known to kill and eat anything. Men. Bears. Pigs. Giraffes. Anything at all, with one exception. For some reason it will not kill and eat an elephant. The problem is most people can't walk around with an elephant on a leash to protect themselves from a manticore.

When I'm in the part of the world where the manticore roams, namely India and Pakistan, I always rent an elephant for the day. Manticores are known to eat more than one person at a time, and I don't want to be the next victim. Between the venom in the tail, the sharp teeth, the speed of a lion, and the human intellect, the manticore is not something I want to mess with. Unlike many other monsters, it's not something I ever want to meet!

PRETA

Pretas are ghosts, but they aren't like the usual kind of ghost. They don't just hang around and scare people. Pretas are much, much worse.

This is a monster with its origins in Buddhism, Hinduism, and Jainism, which are mainly found in India and southeast Asia. These religions teach that if you are kind to all living things in this life, you'll be rewarded in your next life. This is known as "reincarnation," where a person dies but then comes back to live another life, either as a new person or as something else entirely. However, followers of these religions also believe that if you are a mean person in this life, you will be punished after you die. You might not be reincarnated at all.

Or maybe you'll be brought back as a preta, a hungry ghost.

Pretas have no choice but to wander the Earth forever trying to feed an endless hunger. Some of them are even doomed to only eat human poop. Others will eat anything they can find, but there's a catch. These ghosts have a huge, hungry belly, but a very tiny, narrow neck, so they can never get enough into the belly at one time to fill it up. Remember these ghosts are being punished for how they lived their lives, so this is literally a punishment worse than death.

Living relatives of the pretas will sometimes leave out offerings of food for them, in the hopes that they can make the hungry ghost feel just a little bit better. If they don't leave food offerings, the preta is given one day a year to come back in a living body and devour whatever it can from its relatives.

It's better to be safe than sorry, so I left an apple out on the table last night. It was still here this morning, but it did have several tiny teeth marks in it, as if someone with a mouth that was way too small had tried to eat it...

ROMPO

The rompo is a creature that prowls a very large area all around the countryside of India and Africa. I've only seen it a few times, because of how fast it is, and how well it hides. This monster has the head and mouth of a rabbit, but the ears of a human, and a horse's mane for hair. Its front legs look like a badger's but its back legs look like a bear's. Its tail is long and bushy like a fox. No, I don't have photographs. You'll have to take my word for it.

The rompo doesn't like to eat humans—at least, not living ones. This monster digs up dead things that have been buried. It doesn't eat them right away, though. Once it digs up the dead animal—or human—it likes to drag them around in the sun for a few days, letting them rot longer before it starts to feast.

That's how I saw the rompo in the first place. I dug a shallow hole in the ground, and buried myself in it. I waited and, sure enough, the rompo found me and dug me up. It was frightening to be dragged around by the creature for a full day, and not easy to play dead.

That's actually what gave me away. I carefully slid out my cell phone and prepared to take a picture. That was when the rompo realized I was still alive. It screamed at me in a voice I hope to never hear again, and then it ran away. I haven't been back to look for it since.

YETI

Most of us know this monster. He's also known as the Abominable Snowman. He's big, and tall, and covered from head to toe in thick white fur. He usually blends right in to most snowy landscapes. Most people hiking in the Himalayan mountains don't even see the yeti in his natural environment for that very reason. All they see is two black eyes blinking in a snowstorm, or footprints in the snow that are big enough for a small child to lie down in.

The footprints quickly disappear in the snow, just like the yeti. They try to avoid human contact whenever they can.

The Himalayan mountains are in a remote part of India. The terrain is dangerous for hikers like me. Most people never climb here, but I like a challenge. I don't like it so much this time.

Now that I've finally managed to meet a yeti face to face, I can see why people are scared of them. It's the long, sharp teeth. It's the breath that smells like rotten meat. It's the fact that its hands are large enough to wrap around my waist and break me in two, if it wants.

This one wasn't looking to hurt me, though. In fact, he was smiling around those huge, white teeth. He was happy to help me.

I've broken my ankle, and the yeti is carrying me to safety.

You see, sometimes the monsters are the good guys.

MONGOLIAN DEATH WORM

The Mongolian death worm lurks beneath the hot, endless sands of the Gobi Desert in Northern China. This tube-like worm can grow up to three feet long, which is more than half the height of most people. It is a thick, dark red creature with spikes on both sides of its body. Its open, circular mouth has rings of sharp teeth.

In other words, stay away from this thing.

The Mongolian death worm likes to hide under the sand, lying in wait until it feels the vibrations of footsteps walking above. When it knows a victim is near, it will strike, jumping up through the sand and spitting a stream of venom at the person's face. The venom is so strong that it will reportedly kill anyone it touches. These stories are unconfirmed, of course. No one has ever been struck by the monster's venom and lived to tell the tale.

I've set several traps for the worm and all of them have come up empty. In fact, when I went to check on the metal cages I'd set up, many had holes in them. The wire of the cage had been melted away, almost like something had been squirted on it from the inside. Something like a venom that was strong enough to kill anything it touched...and maybe even melt metal. Next time, I'll try flying a drone over the desert to see if I can spot a long tubular worm crawling through the sand.

ALMAS

The almas are a race of monster known as the "Wildmen of Mongolia." They live in caves high up in the mountains of Mongolia, a country that sits on the border of China and Russia. They are human-looking, except for the fact that they are covered in shaggy hair all over their body, except for their wrinkled face and hands. They are also very heavy with muscle and fat, and can weigh up to five hundred pounds.

That's what makes their footprints in the ground so easy to find. Their feet sink into the ground with every step. They can't help but leave a trail everywhere they go. It's helpful to know where they've been...but not very helpful if one is sneaking up behind you.

You might also know they're coming because of the shrill scream they bellow into the air. It echoes off the mountains even from far away. Or, maybe you'll smell their terrible body odor. No matter how many baths they take, they still smell awful. I guess it's all that hair.

The almas are much stronger and faster than ordinary people. They're also very good at climbing, which makes sense, considering they live in the mountains. Today, my path takes me right through those mountains, but I'm prepared for the almas. I'm carrying a pair of scissors. If they don't want a haircut, they'll stay away from me!

NIAN

The nian is a fierce and ancient Chinese monster. Most Chinese monsters are made up of several parts of many different animals, and the nian are no different. They have the head of a lion and the body of a giant dog, with a sharp horn in the middle of their forehead that they use as a weapon.

These monsters live under the sea, but once a year, on the last day of the Chinese calendar year, the nian get hungry. That's when they climb out of the water and make their way toward the villages to hunt. Of course, when a monster comes for you at the same time every year, you can be prepared for it and protect yourself.

Chinese New Year is one of the biggest celebrations in that country. They celebrate it with joyous singing, and parades, and fireworks. In fact, the Chinese invented fireworks, which might have been to protect themselves from the nian! On the very night the nian approach the villages to feed, the Chinese people set off loud, colorful fireworks. They scare the nian right back to the water, where they have to wait for another year before trying again.

So, if you're creating a monster kit to repel monsters, always include a few fireworks in it. You never know what might work.

CHINESE DRAGON

Most of us are familiar with the dragons from the stories of medieval knights. The ones that look like giant, long-necked lizards and breathe fire. Chinese dragons are different. They don't look like anything you've ever seen before.

Some Chinese dragons are long and serpentine, like snakes, with four legs and clawed feet, and a large flat face. They are as big as a house and breathe fire just like the dragons in the rest of the world. Other Chinese dragons have the body of a snake, but the tail of a large fish, the face of a camel, and the clawed feet of a tiger. The odd combination is frightening…and maybe a little funny to look at.

As terrifying as they are, there's one more difference between the Chinese dragon and the dragons from other parts of the world. The Chinese dragon is a gentle monster who only wants to be friends with the smaller humans who live in its territory. In fact, the Chinese consider the dragon to be good luck. These dragons were believed to bring rain to dry lands when they needed it. There's even a legend of a dragon who used his fire-breathing one winter when the Emperor's palace became buried in snow. He melted the snow and freed all the people!

I can also tell you from personal experience that flying on one of these dragons is a thrill. They fly through the air the same way a snake moves on the ground, gliding from side to side, side to side. It's just like riding a rollercoaster! They require a gift whenever they give a human a ride, however. They're partial to fish, in case you ever have the chance to meet one.

THE PACIFIC

KAMA ITACHI

High in the mountains of Japan there are strange little beasts, lurking and waiting for unsuspecting travelers to pass by. The Japanese named them kama itachi, which translates to "sickle weasels." They have spikes on their backs like hedgehogs, and long, super sharp claws shaped like sickles, which is of course where they got their names.

It's also why people try their best to stay away from them.

It is said that these animals travel on the brisk winds that rush down from the tops of their mountain homes. Apparently, they move so fast on these winds that you can't see them. You can only hear them barking like dogs as they fly by. Or, you'll feel them as they cut your skin as they whip past you. They travel in packs of three, and each one has a special role. The first one knocks you down. The second one cuts you with its claws. The third one actually layers a thin sheet of ice over the wound to keep you from feeling the pain.

That explains all the blood on my pants. Next time I'm travelling in the mountains of Japan, I'm going to wear layers of clothing. Enough that even the sharp claws of the kama itachi can't cut through it.

KAPPA

These monsters lives in rivers and ponds in Japan. They are sort of like turtle people, with webbed feet and hands, and shells on their back. The top of their head looks like a bowl, and they carry water in it wherever they go.

Hunting this creature was easy. Although they avoid people, they have a very unpleasant smell, like rotting fish, because they fart constantly. I spent a few days following the majestic rivers in Japan, and found a group of them, skulking and hunting small animals to eat.

Farmers leave gifts for the kappas to keep them happy, and keep them away so they won't eat their crops. They like to do awful things, like drown farm animals, or kidnap and eat people! They prefer cucumbers, according to legend, but they eat human flesh whenever they can. The group I found needs to move on so the farmers and their animals can feel safe. That's why I'm here.

As I got closer, several of the kappa jumped out of the water to fart on me. They like to play tricks like that. I'll shower later but right now I have a trick of my own. If a kappa dumps the water out of their heads, they lose their powers.

With a smile, I held up a bag of cucumbers I had brought for them —their favorite snack. As I handed it to them, I bowed.

When the kappas saw the treat, they all bowed to me in return and dumped all their water out! They ran away screaming and cursing my name. I know they'll want revenge. It might be a good idea for me to stay out of Japan for a while...

PONTIANAK

In Southeast Asia, there is a kind of vampire that is more ghost than flesh-and-blood monster. The Pontianak is the angry spirit of a girl who died when she was still very young, and now is doomed to walk the Earth forever looking for human blood to drink. Animal blood won't do. Her thirst is strictly for human blood.

What's worse, she can change her shape. She usually looks like a beautiful grown woman with long dark hair, and wears a white dress. But she can look like anyone she chooses. Sometimes she chooses to look like her little girl self again. She has been known to imitate friends and family of people to draw them in close so she can attack them and drain their blood.

It is very important to be sure your friends are who they say they are. Ask them questions that only they would know the answers to. Take lots of pictures of them, because even the best shapeshifting monster can't get everything right. Are your friend's eyes the right color? Did your aunt really get a haircut?

It can also become invisible, like a ghost. All the photographs in your cell phone won't help you if it does that!

The only known way to kill a Pontianak is to behead it. This is not easy because it is most often a ghost. The best thing to do is to wait for it to go to sleep. Once it's asleep, you can cut off its head like a real person. Once you identify the Pontianak, watch it carefully until it's asleep…and take care not to fall asleep before it, or you're in big trouble!

YARA-MA-YHA-WHO

Deep in the forests of Australia we find the legendary yara-ma-yha-who. Australia's native peoples knew all about this monster. Over time, tales about it have grown.

It is a creature covered in shaggy red hair, with a huge head that is larger than the rest of its body. Its mouth stretches from ear to ear, big enough to swallow a person whole! There are suckers on its fingers and toes that it uses to drain a victim of blood.

The monster's preferred way of hunting is to latch onto a person with those suckers and drain just enough blood to make the person faint. Once they stop struggling, the yara-ma-yha-who will swallow them up. After that, it does a little dance to help digest its food. Once its eaten, it takes a food nap.

When it wakes up, it vomits up the person it swallowed!

The monster wants to make sure its victim is dead. If the victim is smart, they pretend to be dead while the yara-ma-yha-who pokes them with a stick, tickles them, and does whatever else it can think of to get a response. If the person can pretend to be dead long enough, the monster will leave them alone, and go off to find another victim.

But...if the person so much as twitches, the yara-ma-yha-who swallows them up again, and does its dance again, and goes to sleep again.

I really hope the next time it vomits me up, I can stay perfectly still. It stinks inside this monster, and I'm beginning to feel myself slipping away...

NGAYURNANGALKU

That's a hard one to say, isn't it? Say it like this: "Neh-gay-yure-nan-gal-koo." You might want to practice it a few times. Or, you could just use the translation: "They will eat me."

You're right, the translation is even scarier than their real name. They live in the waters of Lake Kumpupintil, a saltwater lake in Western Australia, also known as Lake Disappointment. This lake has nothing living in it, and often runs dry. All around the lake is a desert, hot and dry, where few things can live. It goes without saying there isn't much food here. In the time of creation, or so the legend goes, cannibal creatures came to live here. Cannibals didn't have to find a lot of food, because they eat their own kind. In this case, their kind was human beings.

They came together around Lake Kumpupintil, and asked one another if they should stop eating their own kind. Many of them stopped, and moved on. The ones who wanted to keep eating human flesh stayed at the lake, and just moved underground. They live in their own realm, where the sun never shines. It caused them to change, until they were all hairless, with huge fangs, and claws on their fingers.

Below the lake, they listen for the sound of footsteps up above. That's when they know a human being is walking around. They wait, and then they spring up from the shallow waters to grab the person and drag them down into their realm, and devour them down to the bones.

Some monsters are better left alone. I think I'll just quietly tiptoe away from Lake Disappointment, and be on my way. They can find someone else to eat.

DAKUWAQA

The Dakuwaqa is an ancient and ferocious sea monster from Fiji, a country made up of a group of islands in the Pacific Ocean. This monster was a giant shark, so massive and scary that it was revered as a god long ago by the people of Fiji. It was a killer, and it took what it wanted, but it also protected the people who swam and fished in the waters around the islands.

Apparently, according to legend, the only god who was ever big enough or fierce enough to defeat Dakuwaqa was an octopus god. The octopus strangled Dakuwaqa with its tentacles, and nearly killed it. The shark god had to plead for its life, and make promises to the octopus in exchange for being given the chance to live. It promised that none of its children would ever bother the people of Fiji who swam in the water. That's why the people in that country can swim in the ocean without fear of being attacked by sharks.

Like most ancient gods in many ancient religions, Dakuwaqa disappeared long ago. No one knows where these monsters go when people stop believing in them. Maybe they were never there. Maybe the monster was real, but the stories were made up. Or maybe I'll take a chance and swim around the islands of Fiji. If I see any sharks, I'll follow them. The shark god might still be hiding deep in the waters off the coast. If it is, other sharks must know about it and could lead me to it.

Made in United States
Troutdale, OR
06/20/2024

20689236R00080